Bicycle Race

Donald Crews

**Greenwillow Books,
New York**

Copyright © 1985 by Donald Crews
All rights reserved.
Manufactured in China.
www.harperchildrens.com

Library of Congress Cataloging
in Publication Data
Crews, Donald. Bicycle race.
"Greenwillow Books."
Summary: The numbered order
of the twelve racers changes as
the bicycle race progresses.
1. Children's stories, American.
[1. Bicycle racing—Fiction.
2. Racing—Fiction]   I. Title.
PZ7.C8682Bi   1985   [E]   84-27912
ISBN 0-688-05171-5
ISBN 0-688-05172-3 (lib. bdg.)

10   First Edition

one

two

three

4 four

5 five

6 six

7 seven

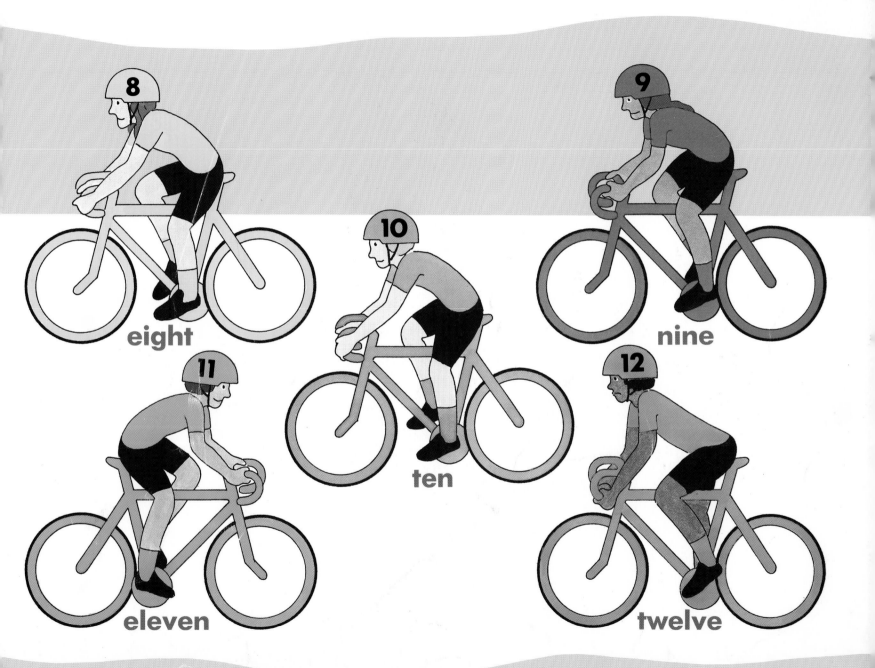

8 eight

9 nine

10 ten

11 eleven

12 twelve

Bicycle race today.

Twelve bicycles, twelve riders.

R E A D Y . . .
S E T . . .

WILL O. GREEN

GO!

Number
nine is
in trouble.

WILL O. GREEN

Who's in front? Who will win?

**Number
nine
needs
repair.**

**eight, one, three, two, ten, six, twelve,
four, seven, five, eleven**

**three, ten, two, twelve, seven,
five, six, eight, one, eleven, four**

Where is
number
nine?

six, three, one, five, eight, ten, seven, two, twelve, four, eleven

Number
nine's
not in
the race.

three, five, six, one, ten, seven, eight, twelve, four, eleven, two

one, three, twelve, five, eight, six, eleven, ten, two, seven, four

There she is. There's number nine!

Go, number nine, go!

three, six, eight, one, four, twelve, ten, five, seven, nine

Who's
in front?
Who
will win?

six, three, two, twelve, eight, seven, four, ten, nine, one

two,
three,
eight,
six,
ten,
twelve,
nine,
seven,
four

Here
they
come!

Who's
in front?
Who will
win?

ten, eight, three, nine